CW00728426

Sherlock Holmes and the Case of the Trigger Warning

ABOUT THE AUTHOR

Bruno Vincent is the author of more than thirty books, which have been translated into fifteen languages. He is best known for the Enid Blyton for Grown Ups series (in which he introduced the Famous Five to the perils of modern life), ten of which were *Sunday Times* bestsellers. He has contributed to serious works about the history of poetry and literature, but has also written humorous books in the voices of Charles Dickens, Prince Harry and Danger Mouse, as well as his own collections of horror stories for children, *Grisly Tales from Tumblewater* and *School for Villains*.

Sherlock Holmes and the Case of the Trigger Warning

BRUNO VINCENT

VIKING

UK | USA | Canada | Ireland | Australia
India | New Zealand | South Africa

Viking is part of the Penguin Random House group of companies
whose addresses can be found at global.penguinrandomhouse.com.

Penguin Random House UK,
One Embassy Gardens, 8 Viaduct Gardens, London SW11 7BW

penguin.co.uk
global.penguinrandomhouse.com

First published 2024
001

Set in 12.5/14.75pt Garamond MT Std
Typeset by Jouve (UK), Milton Keynes
Printed and bound in Great Britain by Clays Ltd, Elcograf S.p.A.

The authorized representative in the EEA is Penguin Random House Ireland,
Morrison Chambers, 32 Nassau Street, Dublin D02 YH68

A CIP catalogue record for this book is available from the British Library

ISBN: 978–0–241–72141–4

Penguin Random House is committed to a
sustainable future for our business, our readers
and our planet. This book is made from Forest
Stewardship Council® certified paper.

TRIGGER WARNING

This book contains depictions of triggers

I

'Watson!' cried Holmes, striding into the study and slamming the door behind him. 'I am outraged!'

'My dear Holmes!' I said, looking up from my papers. 'What has happened?'

'It's this appalling Post Office scandal,' he said. 'You know I cannot abide injustice of any kind! Well, this is an abomination!' He prowled forwards and back, agitation evident in every atom of his being.

'I quite agree,' I said solemnly. 'It is a most awful case . . .'

'Ah, so you know about it, do you?'

'Indeed! One hopes that in time we shall see due reparation . . .'

'I don't understand it,' he muttered. 'I wanted to send one of those electronic letters you told me about. So I printed out the message, took it to the Baker Street Post Office, and do you know what, they refused to send it as a telegram! What do you make of that? It's a disgrace!'

'Holmes . . .'

'You know, it would not surprise me one jot if some of those beastly sub-postmasters turn out to be criminals, stealing for themselves . . .'

'Holmes!' I protested. 'You are quite out of step with the mood of the country!'

'Oh well,' he said, and threw himself onto the chaise

longue. 'I already am in so many other ways, what's one more? You take the side of these scoundrels, do you?'

After calling for tea, I gently explained to my dear friend the details of the *other* (and to his cast of mind, secondary) Post Office scandal which had been gripping the country for many months – perhaps the greatest miscarriage of justice in history. As Mrs Hudson arrived with the tea things, he grudgingly admitted there might be something in it.

'Now Holmes,' I said, pouring him a cup, 'you must try to calm down. Your blood pressure, you see? Speaking as your doctor, you understand . . .'

'Blood pressure can go to blazes,' he said, his eyes flashing. 'There's something far more important afoot. Watson . . . I'm afraid it's time for me to retire!'

2

I did not drop my cup of oolong, but I spilled much of its contents over the latest edition of *The Modern Phrenologist.*

'You don't mean it!' I said, mopping up the mess and returning to my desk.

'And why shouldn't I mean it?' Holmes asked. He stood and walked to the window, where he looked out, giving a pensive and disgusted stare at all the world outside.

'This city has no need for me. Look at Baker Street! I don't recognize it. Baskin-Robbins Ice Cream, Taco Bell, Dunkin' Donuts, KFC! We might as well be in Omaha, Nebraska! And this tea isn't Mrs Hudson's usual brand. Revolting!' He took a sip and flared his nostrils with disdain. 'What are you doing now?'

'I was writing up some notes . . .' I began.

'Well, must you hammer on the keys like a concert pianist? It's impossible for a man to think!'

I let out a deep sigh. My friend the famous consulting detective was a man of passions and moods. Sometimes – when consumed by a case – he did not stir from his couch for weeks on end. At other times, when on the scent of a culprit, he could survive on barely any sleep for days and was the most animated individual in the universe. He was absolute in all things – which meant when he felt in the doldrums, we all felt it with him.

'You've been worrying me recently, my dear Holmes,' I said. 'That you are perhaps a tad depressed.'

To my surprise, he did not explode with temper. Instead he turned, and in a mournful confiding tone, asked: 'Who *wouldn't* be depressed, Watson? Not a single case for four months! Sixteen agonizing weeks of inactivity without – mind you! – being allowed a single pipe, cigarette or cigar! And these blasted nicotine patches don't help a jot . . .'

'I feel it too,' I said. 'Why, what about last week when the tea cosy went missing? That was a tricky mystery, was it not? To rival the case of the Red-Headed League!'

'I am not so reduced in capacity, Watson, so as not to feel patronized by your hiding the tea cosy and seeing if I could locate it.'

'I'll say you're not reduced in capacity!' I said. 'You found it in fifteen minutes flat!'

'Hiding it under the bearskin cap of one of the guards at Buckingham Palace was just insulting. To me *and* him. We were lucky not to be arrested!'

'Had to call in a few favours, it's true,' I admitted. 'But I was just desperate to get you out of the house and distract you from your nicotine withdrawal.'

'No, dear friend,' said the great detective, his energy suddenly leaving him, 'I feel it *is* time to retire – rather than dying here by slow hours, waiting and hoping for the world to remember me . . .'

3

'What is that?' Holmes asked. I had roused him from his lethargy by waving an envelope in the air.

'I feared you had come to some such conclusion, Holmes,' I said. 'And so I wrote to an old acquaintance in the country, asking if we might take a few days to breathe the fresh air of the great outdoors and forget our worries.'

'I never take holidays,' he said flatly. 'They are for the feeble-minded and the French. I am neither.'

'I knew you felt that way,' I said. But I could not contain my grin. 'Which was why I felt so amazed when I received this reply . . .'

He sipped his tea and regarded me sceptically, offering no encouragement.

'I shall read it to you,' I said.

' "My dear Dr Watson, many greetings from Baskerville Hall. Your letter arrived with miraculous timing, for a terrible thing has happened. Or rather – a sequence of terrible things. The Hall has been the scene of a number of violent and horrible incidents, leading to my receiving today a direct threat on our lives here. The motive is bewildering; the effect has been devastating. I beg you to come at once. I feel convinced something truly awful is about to happen – and that the curse of the Baskervilles has returned! Yours, B. Sholdsmith." '

I glanced up from the letter. 'What do you make of

that?' I looked around the room for a moment. There was no one there. 'Holmes?'

He appeared at the door. His hat was on his head, his coat over his arm, his stick in one hand. And on the face that look of fierce alive determination which warmed my heart.

'What are we waiting for, Watson?'

I held up my phone and peered at the Uber app, where a miniature black car was awkwardly turning a corner onto a map of Baker Street. 'Um, someone called Piotr. He is apparently three minutes away.'

'Bravo!' Holmes exclaimed jubilantly.

4

The journey to Grimpen railway station in Devonshire afforded Holmes and myself much time for reminiscence of old cases and excited speculation as to the current events at Baskerville. Rather more time than necessary, in fact, due to the planned engineering works between Westbury and Taunton, an apparently unplanned staff shortage which delayed the connecting train, and the vanishing scarcity of the rail replacement bus service which was needed to bring us the final twelve miles to Grimpen, where at last we arrived.

At first appearance the village was miraculously unchanged: streets of beautiful stone dwellings and picturesque gardens in full flower, surrounded by the vibrant fecundity of the English country summer, and all around us the buzzing and tweeting of irrepressible nature.

'Blasted pollen,' said Holmes, sneezing, as we stepped from the bus with our suitcases.

The extra three hours on top of the already lengthy journey had done nothing to improve his mood. Having completed his book of Killer Sudoku (while I soldiered on through my copy of *Murdle*), at last he had lapsed into moody silence. I perceived I had my work cut out for me.

'This suitcase barks my shins – how I mourn the decline of the English porter! Where's our hotel, Watson?'

He marched over the road to the local inn and,

dropping his suitcase at the door, smartly requested a small boy at a nearby table to look after it if he wanted a shilling. The boy's parents looked up, alarmed, but the lad's eyes did not leave his tablet.

'No hotels round here, the barman says!' Holmes called from the bar.

'Council's got 'em full up of illegal immigrants,' said a customer. He was one of a party of four, all looking flushed with a mix of emotion and the local cider.

'There's a protest about it tomorrow,' said the woman next to him. 'It's disgusting what they're doing . . .'

'No matter,' said Holmes. 'I'm sure Watson's booked into one of your charming local bed and breakfasts . . .'

With difficulty I extricated my friend from an increasingly uncomfortable discussion and explained to him during the half-hour wait for a taxi that, although we were to stay at a beautiful traditional cottage off the beaten track, mention of the Airbnb booking service often caused local tempers to fray.

'. . . and round here tempers are pretty close to snapping already,' he observed.

'So it seems!' I agreed. 'I wonder if this tension and the troubling developments at the old Hall are connected . . .'

5

The taxi took us down a rutted path to a whitewashed thatched cottage which squatted behind a high hedgerow enclosing an enchanting garden of wildflowers, fruit trees and, in the far corner, a cluster of beehives.

In only a quarter of an hour the two of us managed to unlock the key box by the front door, and after consulting the four-page rulebook on the kitchen table, and managing to work the Wi-Fi password ('prettyflyforaWiFi', which caused Holmes's teeth to grind), and making a restorative cup of tea (Fortnum's lapsang souchong, which appeased his irritation), we discovered it was nearly ten p.m. A visit to Baskerville Hall was clearly best left until the morning, so we retired.

The following day, therefore, we presented ourselves at nine sharp outside the Hall grounds.

'Brings back memories,' he said.

'Does it not, Holmes,' I said. 'One of your greatest cases!'

'One of *our* greatest, surely, Watson,' he gently corrected me. 'Although for my part I mainly remember being chased by dogs, covered in soaking mud, and spending several weeks hiding in a stone cottage in near-freezing temperatures.'

'No Airbnb in those days, sadly . . .' I lamented. 'But here now, what's this?'

We had been walking towards the massive entry gates to the Hall, which were still magnificently ornate: wild curlicues of wrought iron between two stone posts on which stood the carved heads of two giant wild boar – the emblem of the Baskerville family.

Beyond this, nothing was the same.

It might perhaps be admitted that the *skeleton* of the old building remained; just about discernible among the riot of alteration that surrounded it. The walls had been painted bright colours. Annexes, addendums and appendices sprouted on each side: wonderful to behold but mysterious of purpose.

The gardens had previously been a formal and sober affair, appropriate to a large private house. Now they were joyous and sprawling, with animal coops and vegetable plots giving on to serried beds of blooming exotic flowers, ranks of motorized sprinklers swishing peacefully, colourful trails of solar-powered fairy lights, greenhouses like mighty scientific laboratories of nurture and nature.

Holmes and I stood for a long moment, wondering.

Above us on the high stone wall where once had stood a severe rust-blackened sign reading 'Baskerville Hall', there was now a six-foot colourful banner-map of the surrounding countryside showing natural points of interest both inside the grounds and out, with illustrations and descriptions of local animals and indications of where they could be spotted, and a helpful 'you are here' at the bottom. At the top were the words 'BASKERVILLE ECO-EXPERIENCE'.

'Hang on, they've got the *X Factor* final on.'
'I tell you, Holmes, we are perfectly able to afford a television set of our own!'

And across this, someone had freshly sprayed in red a crude skull and crossbones, alongside the word 'MURDERES!!!'

Holmes and I looked at each other. Then we both looked back at the word, scrawled in a rough and shaky hand. The paint appeared so fresh it seemed almost still to be drooling down the map's surface.

'Now *this* promises to be interesting,' said Sherlock Holmes.

6

We announced ourselves at the entryphone, and the gates buzzed then swung judderingly open.

The gardens proved no less splendid and impressive as we walked the gravel path to the front entrance, and Holmes and I marvelled at the changes we saw in every direction. The door opened as we approached and we were met by a friendly and intelligent-looking woman of about five-and-thirty who welcomed us and then, her feelings getting the better of her, took our hands and shook them warmly.

'Mr Holmes – welcome to the Baskerville Eco-Experience!'

'I am *so* grateful – so very grateful – to you for coming. I am Bernie Sholdsmith – do come in . . . I'll put the kettle on . . .'

Those last words sounded peculiar as she retreated into the vast central hall of Baskerville, whose austere magnificence could not be concealed or altered by the colourful decorations. One constantly expected a host of employees to surge into sight from every direction.

There was a gift shop to one side of the broad reception, featuring a large information point called 'Askerville!' On the other side was a café (adorned with deep sofas and a neon sign that throbbed the word 'RELAX' in fuchsia) named Baskers, although no one happened to be basking at that moment in the sunlight cascading through the medieval stained-glass windows.

In fact, no one was to be seen anywhere.

Bernie took us past reception and up one half of the twin staircases that rose to the colonnaded gallery, then we followed her clattering heels along the wood-floored corridor to her office.

A kettle rumbled in the corner of the room while she repeated her fulsome thanks – but Holmes cut this off soon enough.

'There is much to interest me in this case. Not only my – my and Watson's I mean *our* – history with the place, but also what we've seen so far today. Most urgently however, madam, please share with us this death threat you received.'

Bernie took a heavy breath and nodded. Then sat at her desk and, opening the top drawer, pulled out an envelope. Holmes and I peered at it – it was addressed to her in person, in shaky block capitals, deliberately styled to mask the author's true handwriting. With a pen she flicked open the flap and then tilted the envelope upside down.

Onto the table rattled a small curved piece of metal, straight on one edge.

'It appears to be the trigger of a gun,' said Holmes.

'The meaning is clear,' said Bernie. 'There was nothing else in the envelope – except this.'

She prised back the flap again and we saw written clearly on its inside:

BEWARE

7

'How awful!' I said.

'Decidedly unpleasant,' agreed Holmes.

'Please, allow me . . .' I said, walking to the kettle and busying myself among the cups and saucers. 'You just tell us everything that has happened . . .'

Holmes folded his hat and, putting it in his pocket, sat at a chair in front of her desk, frowning with concentration. Ms Sholdsmith sighed, no doubt wondering where to begin.

'It all started – oh, a month or so ago.'

'The precise date, please,' said Holmes.

Bernie thought. 'The twenty-seventh of May,' she said. 'I opened up that morning.'

'No one stays overnight on site, then?'

'Not until the summer holidays, when we have star-spotting sessions – and we have a dozen yurts, of course, which get hired out for various uses.'

' "Glamping", I believe is the phrase?' asked Holmes, and I saw the muscles in his jaw flex as he repressed a grimace.

'That's right,' said Bernie.

'An admirable idea!' I said. 'Milk, sugar?'

'Watson, you know full well it is not appropriate to call a young woman "sugar". Apologize at once!'

'Holmes!' I protested.

'Just my little joke, Watson,' he said, although his expression lost none of its customary sternness. 'I have read that it helps to relieve tension in social situations. Coffee for me, no sugar, as you know . . .'

Bernie requested a tea with one-and-a-quarter sugars, plus the tiniest bit extra – a quarter of a quarter – and watched approvingly as I made the measurements as precisely as though labouring over a chemistry set. Then, while I served up, with a few false starts and some nervous pauses – and apologizing for being a stickler about the amount of sugar in her tea – the whole story came out.

'I've been the manager here for two years . . .'

'You are not, then, yourself a Baskerville?'

'Oh, dear me no,' she said, and almost seemed amused at the idea. 'Your original letter, Dr Watson, was addressed to one of my predecessors, but found its way to me and I took the liberty of replying to you, as it seemed like manna from heaven. No – I'm no Baskerville by name, but have fallen in love with the place since I was awarded this post and moved to the area. And while I admit the famous curse is good for tourism, I never gave it the slightest credit. You wouldn't, would you?'

'Would we, Watson?' asked Holmes.

I stirred my tea and refused to meet his eye. 'My dear – do you actually know the story of the curse?'

'Um, vaguely,' she said, leaning back in her chair. 'It's to do with that awful git, isn't it?'

She pointed at an oil portrait over the mantelpiece which had so far evaded Holmes's and my notice, because it had various Post-its on it bearing phone numbers and aides-memoires, and also a clipboard leaning against it with the legend 'LEST WE FORGET' written in dramatic capitals, beneath which were the council's recycling collection dates.

'Tell her, Watson?'

'Well,' I said, nibbling a Garibaldi and tucking it back onto my saucer. 'The curse was placed upon Sir Hugo, who was lord here in 1649, I think . . .'

'1647,' said Holmes quietly. He had his fingers steepled and his eyes closed in concentration while he listened.

'1647, quite right,' I agreed. 'He was a villain, who with his drunken companions kidnapped a local girl for his own . . .'

'. . . rapey . . . intentions?' Bernie suggested.

'Yes, not the word I would have chosen but . . . sadly, accurate. Before he could . . . you know . . . she escaped across the moor and he set off in pursuit, offering to sell his soul to the devil in order to catch her. Catch her he did – but at the same time a hound came out of the fog and ripped his throat out!'

'Good thing too,' said Bernie.

'A "hound of hell" was the local legend.'

'And it came back? Right? Last time you two visited?'

Holmes harrumphed. 'Certainly not. It was the work of a nasty specimen called Stapleton, who used the legend to scare the then Lord Baskerville to death with a – well – a big dog he brought down from London.'

'Down from London?' said Bernie. 'Worst thing you can be in the country, a DFL.'

'So the dog was a *D*DFL,' said Holmes.

'But the locals, of course, remained superstitious,'

I said. 'They felt the curse was still in place. I trust they are a less credulous bunch these days?'

Now it was Ms Sholdsmith's turn to harrumph. 'I wouldn't be too sure. They're always in uproar about something, jumping at ghosts, thinking that there is an invasion of immigrants or millionaire hedge-fund managers taking away their god-given rights. Believing in a cursed hound of hell about to commit murder – I wouldn't put it past them at all!'

8

'Thank you for giving me the full version,' said Bernie. 'It's all bollocks of course – a fairy tale. But it helps us no end with our mission here at Baskerville.'

'Which is?' asked Holmes.

She looked at him in surprise. 'Everything you see around you. These old properties are ruinously expensive to run, with a great deal of revenue needed to keep them going. It's a constant worry, and getting worse every day. I started working at National Heritage with a mission to prove that they can be made good for the environment, for locals, and be totally self-sustaining.'

She rose and went to the window, beckoning us to follow. She started to point out various areas on the grounds.

'All our packaging and cutlery is biodegradable. There's the composting toilets, which help keep our plants growing year-round on the rather rocky and inhospitable soil in this part of the world. All the food we serve is grown here. We are as close to a zero-waste facility as possible, with our energy coming from ground-source heat pumps.

'If this project works, it could be rolled out across the country. Many rural communities like this one could be helped to keep going, and many precious buildings saved from total destruction.'

'The building is *somewhat* changed from its original appearance,' I suggested.

'This was not at all what I expected from a "luxury rustic annex", Watson.'

She nodded. 'That's true – but there must be some trade-offs. Since these changes, visitors have increased five-fold and numbers are continuing to grow year on year. We have yoga classes – five different types – knit-along-a-*Sound-of-Music*, glamping in the summer, a farming museum, foraging courses for all ages, and over a hundred school visits a year, where pupils learn about sustainability and wildlife. And we are the number one destination for same-sex weddings and civil partnerships in the West Country – some people think because of the pink hue of the local stone from which the house was constructed.'

Holmes nodded. 'Makes sense. You've made it so bright, beautiful, friendly – a delightfully gay place!'

'So much colour,' I agreed. 'And a marked improvement on the dour old pile we remember, eh, Holmes?' He assented readily.

'But all these changes were hugely expensive. We're talking millions. National Heritage will never attempt this again if it doesn't work, so it *must* work. So much depends on it. And it *was* working . . .'

'Until the twenty-seventh of May,' suggested Holmes.

'Yes,' she said. 'When the threats started.'

9

'First, there was a smashed window. An old leather boot thrown through the stained glass.'

'Expensive to repair?' I asked.

'Ruinously so.'

'A piece of casual vandalism?' Holmes asked.

Bernie shook her head. 'The grounds are covered by CCTV. This person managed to throw the boot from outside the property, just at the point where the cameras couldn't see them. There are thirty windows closer and easier to hit from the spot where it was thrown. I went and stood there, and counted them. What's worse – it is part of the fabric of the original building and must be remade in accordance with the original materials. Only one place in Britain still makes those, a specialist in Durham. As I said – ruinously expensive.'

'*Not* casual, then, but focused and deliberate violence,' said Holmes. 'Interesting. May I see the boot?'

She blinked at him. 'I never thought . . . I think I threw it away.'

'A pity,' he said, 'but of course you never knew it was the first of many such attacks. What happened next?'

'A fire. In the old chapel.'

'There's a chapel?' I asked. 'I thought the Baskervilles were a rather godless breed . . .'

'Well, it's a table-tennis room now, and part-time repair shop.' She pointed it out to me. 'Or it was until the fire.'

'Let me guess. Original materials were damaged again?'

She nodded. 'The exterior Tudor oak beams were wrecked.'

Although the tale was a woeful one, I could see it was a relief to her to find herself being closely quizzed by the great Sherlock Holmes. She stood taller, as though weight was steadily being lifted from her shoulders with each inquiry. It did me good to see it.

'There have been other instances – luckily not so severe, and disaster was averted. I thought there was a chance we might get through this. But my staff have been resigning in droves. They all have different excuses, but basically I know they're spooked. And I get it. Of course they would be – after all, it has been part of my mission to employ vulnerable people who struggle to find work, to give them opportunities and help the community.' She sighed. 'If it's death threats now, that will be the end. This place will close forever, and scotch the chances of any others like it in the future.

'Unless, of course, there's anything *you* can do, Mr Holmes!'

10

'You've spoken to the police?' I asked.

At this, all the weight returned to Ms Sholdsmith's shoulders.

'I . . .' She hesitated. 'I am deeply averse to the danger of bad publicity. I've done no more than make a report for insurance purposes. I'm afraid that is what the miscreants want – bad word to spread about this place. Then the writing really will be on the wall . . .'

She was undoubtedly in a tight spot. And perhaps it was possible that the curse of the Baskervilles – if indeed such a fanciful thing existed – was directed at the inhabitants of the Hall and not the family descendants.

At her reference to 'writing on the wall', Holmes and I gave her the grim tidings of the message scrawled at the front gate. Her face fell, and she made a call. When she hung up, she looked exhausted and baffled.

'Do you have any idea who is doing all this, and why?' I asked.

She returned to the window. 'Out there.' She pointed. 'Until today, all the damage has been on *that* side of the property, which faces the moor. It's weird. There's no access to that land from the road – it's fenced off. To approach the property from that side would be . . .' She hesitated. 'To get there you'd have to go miles and miles out of your way. It feels like it's someone who lives out there on the moor – which adds to the spookiness of it.'

'Found you.'
'I have not even started hiding, Watson!'

'And as to motive?' Holmes asked.

She looked at him and seemed to choose her words carefully. 'I don't *know* why . . . but there is one last thing I should show you . . .'

A few minutes later we were walking through the southward-facing rear garden of the estate. It was even more varied and impressive than its front equivalent, and we would not have noticed anything amiss if Ms Sholdsmith had not pointed it out to us.

Right against the boundary wall was a tall stone plinth, with a large plant pot on top. Our host showed us where the wall had been wrecked and then temporarily mended with wooden planks. The plinth was damaged too, one side of it scraped and chipped to a depth of six inches, from what must have been an exceptionally heavy blow.

'What happened here?' Holmes inquired.

'Here is where a statue of Sir Charles stood, until two weeks ago. It was pulled down in the middle of the night . . .'

'*Pulled* down?' I asked. 'By main force?'

'I can't tell you more than that, when we arrived the following morning, it had fallen and crushed the wall. Bear in mind it's stone – weighs over two tonnes. Again, nothing was recorded on camera. One other thing – the graffiti, also on the moor-facing wall. Three times this past month . . .'

She held out her phone and swiped between pictures.

'SLAVE TRADERS', 'BLOOD ON YOUR HANDS' and 'YOU'RE ON THE WRONG SIDE OF HISTORY'. In the final two pictures, rusted chains had been draped across the top of the wall, hanging down over the words and giving the striking impression of a medieval torture dungeon.

Holmes's eyes narrowed. 'Are those words written . . .'

'In oil,' she said, nodding. 'Had to get a specialist from Widecombe to wash it off. Then there were the chains – god, I nearly fainted when I saw those . . .'

'Where did our assailant get such chains, do you think?' Holmes asked.

'There are lots of derelict buildings among the woods nearby – the Baskerville estate has varied in size over the centuries. Many of them contain abandoned farm machinery, and anyone who wants to cut through the overgrowth could go in there and dig it out, if they're motivated. I'm pretty sure they came from there. But . . .' She shrugged.

Her hand holding out the device trembled. Now she put it away, defeated. 'I don't feel we *are* on the wrong side of history. Of course I don't. I mean, who *could* feel that way . . .'

'Naturally,' I agreed. But nothing we said could shake the poor woman's haunted look.

She glanced out at the moor. 'There's something out there – something like fate – and it feels like it's got it in for me . . .'

11

At the gate, Holmes and I waited for the local taxi service, which consisted of a jolly man named Ted, who was extremely reliable – being always exactly thirty minutes late.

'I am not *uber*-fond of this chap,' muttered Holmes, looking at his watch as the car parked across the road from us gave a cheery honk. 'If you get my drift.'

The car delivered us to Grimpen village, where we intended to continue our investigations.

'Where first, Holmes?'

'Well, Watson, the thatched cottage is marvellously comfortable and I had an excellent night's sleep. But I'm not bowled over by the generosity of the *second* "b" in Airbnb. Breakfast ought to consist of more than a muffin and half a carton of "Best-Valu" orange juice. A bit early for lunch, but I'm ravenous. Let us retire to that rather charming traditional-looking inn. A hub of local information, I'll wager!'

On entering the pub for the second time, we had a chance to look around us and properly take it in. The publican, a stout and ruddy-faced individual, sat us in a corner near the fireplace.

Gradually locals drifted in, filling up the tables around us: a most unpretentiously dressed crowd of farm labourers, shop workers and white-haired retirees.

'Look, Watson – a good old-fashioned local newspaper! Didn't know these still existed!' He plucked the said item off a shelf and leafed hungrily through it while I looked about the place. A theme quickly emerged.

'All the clues to the crime are to be found in the local newspaper, Watson. See if you can spot them.'
'I see that Miss Murgatroyd is having a jam sale. Perhaps that furnishes us with a motive?'
Holmes sighed.

On the walls were many pictures of large dogs. Hounds, all of them, I was pretty sure. In one corner was a Hound of Hell-themed fruit machine whose lights twinkled in yellow and red as they merrily lit the phosphorus-covered dog and the pool of blood around the agonized victim at its feet.

'Not in the *very* best taste,' I muttered. And then I recognized the background tune which was now on its third rotation at the mini-jukebox on the pub counter: 'Hound Dog' by Mr E. Presley.

Above our seats, beside an enormous shotgun which hung on the wall over the fireplace, was a wooden board bearing a leather collar. A sign proclaimed it had been 'torn from the throat of the murderous hound by a brave local'.

'I wonder if that could possibly be real . . .' I said, peering at it.

'Only if the genuine hound's name was "Mr Snugglewuggle", Watson,' said Holmes without looking up from his newspaper. 'Look closely.'

'Ah . . .' I did so, and saw that very name etched on the silver medallion that hung from the collar.

'This place has rather gone all in on the tourist trade based on the legend, it seems . . .' I said.

'Yes. It makes one wonder,' said Holmes, looking up at last, 'whether they have strong feelings about the renovation and "re-imagining", I believe people say these days, of Baskerville Hall. Ah! Our pies!'

The landlord was leaning over our table, two steaming plates in hand, but Holmes's words made him stop. 'I wouldn't go up to the Hall if you paid me,' he said. 'If

I wasn't carrying food in both me hands, I'd spit. Now – one chicken and leek, one beef and Stilton?'

'Not a fan of the changes at Baskerville, I take it?' Holmes asked in a voice deliberately raised to ring across the room. Several heads turned, and not one of them was smiling.

'Terrible stuff, what they're doing . . . raking up the past like that . . .' said an elderly woman at a nearby table.

'Oh, please – do tell. I'm most interested. I thought the Hall was a largely beneficial and good-hearted enterprise!'

This was met with a chorus of grumbles.

'These protests,' said a rather weather-beaten man on an adjacent table. 'They make us all look bad.'

Holmes had the attention of the whole pub now, and all of a sudden, in that cosy leather-and-oak cocoon, there was a single conversation. He was right – the locals most certainly had plenty to say.

'They say the family made its money from the slave trade,' said one man. 'It's just terrible.'

'Who says?' asked Holmes.

'I read it on Facebook,' said another. 'There's lots on there. You just look!'

'It's the "Just Stop Oil" people,' said another. 'They've done their research. I wouldn't put anything past these toffs, with their investments that damage the planet . . .'

'There's no smoke without fire, after all,' said someone else, which was greeted with loud assent from around the room.

'But it's owned by National Heritage, surely,' laughed Holmes. 'It has no connection with the family at all!'

No one seemed to have an answer to this, nor did it assuage their suspicions.

'They have a very determined policy of diversity hiring, I understand . . .' prompted Holmes, and I inwardly winced, fearing where the conversation would go next. But I needn't have worried.

'We've got no problem with *that*,' said the landlord, who was back behind the bar pouring a cider. 'My nephew Trevor, who lost his arm when he was a kid, couldn't get a job for years – they got him working in the kitchen. And Pamela over there, her daughter's got brittle bone disease. They employed her too. Done *wonders* for her confidence – right, Pam? Changed her life.' A woman in the far corner nodded emphatically. 'But they can't keep their staff, can they?'

'The younger generation,' suggested Holmes. 'Struggling to stick at things?'

'Oh no,' said the old lady who had spoken earlier. 'They won't tell their bosses this – they make up any old excuse – no. It's because of the hound. It's back, and they've *all seen it*.'

'Prowling around,' said another. 'As fierce-looking as ever. There's bound to be an attack any minute now, then we'll all be sorry. They should shut that place once and for all. It's cursed, plain and simple.'

A horrible silence descended over the room, while everyone considered this ghastly possibility.

Then a hideous roar split the air.

Everybody in the room jumped, and not a few glasses rattled, as the jukebox begged to know (at ear-splitting volume) who precisely it was who had let the dogs out.

'Charming musical accompaniment,' said Holmes, clapping me hard on the back to dislodge the mouthful of chicken pie that had got stuck in my windpipe. 'You see, the jukebox *did* have more than one song all along, Watson!'

12

'Utter and complete horseshit,' said Madeleine Critchley, smiling. 'There's nothing in it.'

'There's a frank answer for you, Watson!' said Holmes.

I blushed, and pretended not quite to have heard.

Ms Critchley was proudly showing us around her garden, where she housed a variety of most of the endangered species to be found on Dartmoor.

It was a fascinating and educational tour. She had shown us the pond, which boasted pool frogs and natterjack toads, and was occasionally visited by bitterns, Eurasian beavers and the chequered skipper butterfly. Now she pointed to the cluster of trees and outhouses where she said she had recently spotted an enigmatic ladybird spider.

'That's nearly every endangered species of Dartmoor, all in my little garden. Aren't I lucky?'

I turned to cast my gaze over her pretty red-brick cottage, daintily veined with ivy and flowering clematis, and with a handwritten placard proclaiming 'BE NICE' from an upstairs window.

'But to return to your previous remark,' urged Holmes. 'About the Baskerville family.'

'Oh that,' she said. 'Yeah, that's just crap. Poor Bernie Sholdsmith is letting some bully get into her head.'

'The locals believe it too . . .'

'But it's all just gossip,' she said. She knelt and peered into the pond, gently stirring the lily pads, as though discussion of the local populace's credulity made her think of pond life. Now she rose and took off her gardening gloves.

On leaving the Hound Inn, Holmes and I had wanted to refresh our knowledge of Dartmoor and had been directed to visit this kindly resident, well known as an irrepressible enthusiast of local history and lore. Such she had proven, even if she only wanted to show us her garden.

'Listen, don't get me wrong,' she said. 'There are *certainly* connections between many English country houses – many National Heritage properties too – and the evils of the past. It's very well documented. Houses built from the proceeds of slavery, from crops like cotton, tobacco, sugar . . . And – whether you agree with their methods or not – people are increasingly protesting to try to make these places acknowledge the past. But Baskerville . . .' She shook her head, baffled. 'It doesn't add up. By the standards of the British gentry, the Baskervilles are tame. Practically church mice. It's been all they can do to keep the roof over their heads for the last four hundred years – there's certainly no connection to the slave trade. Nor oil, as far as I'm aware. They were never very wealthy . . .'

'You know the family history, then?' asked Holmes.

Ms Critchley looked up at the sky, trying to recall precise details. 'Sir Ridley and Lady Evelyn Baskerville were given modest grants by Elizabeth I. She was a lady-in-waiting, or a minor courtier, I think. He was a knight at the time of the Spanish Armada. Which fizzled out disappointingly. Like my gladioli – look! I just cannot make them flower.'

'Sir Hugo was a notorious villain . . .' I put in.

'Yeah, but was he, though? There's no *contemporaneous* proof of all that guff about a hound. First written accounts date from 1742, nearly a hundred years later. Chances are it was a story made up by locals to frighten their daughters to stay indoors, or some later lord improvised it to make his family sound more jazzy and exciting. Are you *sure* I can't interest you in some more cakes? I've made lots . . .'

This extraordinary woman had met us at the door in steamed-up spectacles and oven gloves, having just taken a tray of exquisite fancies out of the oven, and set tea for us at a pretty table beside the pond. By now, Holmes and I had already consumed our daily calorific intake in fairy cakes, millefeuilles and macaroons (all delicious), and now we demurred, to Madeleine's disappointment. She ate one herself, and while she considered what to say next, took a teaspoon-and-a-quarter of sugar for her tea, plus a tiny bit more.

'Now, Sir Charles, you see,' she said through a mouthful of cream and pastry, 'was the *opposite* of Sir Hugo. Charles was a positive sweetie. Was a Liberal MP, supported local causes, invested in the village and the land around here. Everywhere you look there's something named in his honour. That's why it never made sense that a "hound of hell" would attack him – as, indeed, you two proved it didn't. But the superstition sticks, you see. He *was* attacked by a dog, just as Hugo was, and therefore he was probably guilty of something. That's how the imagination of the mob works.'

Holmes and I took all this in for a moment.

'And since Sir Charles's death?'

'Well, there it gets into more of a grey area,' she admitted. 'The most recent heir was a – a bit of a chip off the Hugo block, if you see what I mean. An Eton-educated entitled bully, by all accounts. Sandhurst College, then dishonourably discharged from the army during Afghanistan – wonder what he could have managed to do during that shitshow to get specially noticed. Makes your hair curl just thinking about it. Then did some dodgy contract work abroad for some decidedly unpleasant people. The sort who make the Wagner Group look like the Citizens Advice Bureau. He's a – uh . . .' She paused, looking for the right word.

'A thoroughgoing scoundrel,' I said. 'A rotten egg.'

' "A massive twat" was the phrase I was reaching for,' said that admirably forthright woman. 'But he was never exactly *hated* round here, though, because he never *was* here – grew up at boarding school, lived in Mayfair – so no one knew him to look at, nor really cared. Except that he let the Hall go to rack and ruin.'

'What happened to him?'

'He went missing on a business trip to the Middle East fifteen years ago. His luck ran out, people think. He was declared legally dead recently and that's when National Heritage got its mitts on the Hall – which I think any sensible person would agree was a good thing. Until all this business started.'

'This is all most helpful,' I said. 'And the present heir?'

'It's slightly complicated. He had already disinherited his son, who went to Asia to become a monk in a temple on a mountain somewhere. The Hall eventually fell to his sister's family – who flogged it to National Heritage. Current heir still lives round here, in fact . . .' And she named an address which was just a short stroll from where Holmes and I were staying.

'And so, where do you think these threats have come from?' I inquired.

We had reached the very back of her garden, where the trees parted and a wire fence gave a wide and splendid view of the rugged moor: a dozen miles or so of rock-strewn hills, handsome and lonely.

'It is a harsh, ancient place,' she said. 'You know why I live here? Animals are nicer than people – more sincere – and this place is filled with amazing animals. I don't think I like humans very much at all, you see. And that's the downside of the moor – it attracts strange people, dangerous people . . .'

She paused and, looking into the distance, seemed for a moment transported. As though on the verge of an admission, or a revelation.

'It doesn't matter how grown-up and sensible you think you are, every time you look at it you always feel a sense of something *out* there,' she said. 'Something primal and powerful . . .'

13

'So, you don't know, is basically what you are saying,' said Holmes.

'Yup, that's about the size of it. Now are you *sure* I can't interest you in an Eccles cake?'

We thanked Ms Critchley, and made our excuses. It being a fine afternoon, rather than wait the requisite thirty minutes for Ted's cab, we decided to walk back to our accommodation. The bright sun, and a pleasant breeze, and the apparent lifting of Holmes's spirits combined to make for a pleasant journey for us both.

'Good to have your teeth into a juicy case again, Holmes?' I ventured.

'No pun intended, Watson?'

'Oh, ah – indeed not.'

'Well, I'll admit to you. It was fun while it lasted. But all too easy, I'm afraid.'

'What! You mean you've solved the thing already?'

'Yes indeed. The solution to the mystery occurred to me within two minutes of sitting at our table at the Hound Inn. It is simple enough,' he said. 'The information needed to solve it is contained on pages four, seven and thirteen of the local rag.' He slapped the newspaper across my breast and I opened it, seeking with interest.

'I fail to see what a cake sale to raise funds for a new water fountain at the primary school can teach us . . .'

'Keep looking.'

I flicked some pages. 'Ah – the Dartmoor Badgers Under-15s have been promoted to League Seven of the West Country Softball League. Does that somehow provide a motive?'

He sighed and regarded me drolly. 'While I wait for you to catch on, there was something I thought we might discuss. What do you think that the threat meant, which Ms Sholdsmith showed us this morning?'

'The trigger?' I considered. 'That someone wants to shoot her – or, no, that someone wants her to *think* they intend to.'

'Hmm. By taking the part of the gun necessary to make it fire and sending it to her, though?'

'In these parts, I daresay there are lots of broken old shotguns lying around. And it obviated the need to spell the threat out. Perhaps the police wouldn't take it so seriously. The meaning was clear, but the threat was not *specifically* articulated.'

'A good theory, by Jove! But perhaps there is a metaphorical aspect. What do you understand by the phrase "trigger warning", Watson?'

I ruminated. 'It began as a technical term in the field of psychology, I think – a warning to sufferers of severe trauma, to protect them from experiencing horrific memories again. Let's say, because they run into similar circumstances. If you were trampled by an elephant, then catching sight of an elephant in the flesh would naturally bring that awful memory back.'

'Or, indeed, attacked by a large hound,' said Holmes

thoughtfully. 'Yes. That's how I understood the phrase as well.'

'But the definition has broadened out in recent times. Although "trigger warning" still refers to those very serious cases, it also means alerting audiences of all kinds to terms one might find merely upsetting or distasteful. To help people with specific sensitivities.'

'Funny how "sensitivity" and "intolerance", formerly opposites, are now so close in meaning,' Holmes said, his stick swiping at the bracken. 'You noticed what it said on the menu at the Hound? "Please inform us if you have any intolerances." More than a few among that clientele, I fear. That's what this is, Watson, I think: a case of sensitivities and intolerances.'

We walked on in silence, while Holmes ruminated. 'It's like being in the Wild West,' he said at last.

'Yes!' I agreed heartily. 'I adore Devonshire. Better than stuffy old London. A bit of fresh air . . .'

'No, Watson – forgive me. I meant modern life. It really feels like we are back in a time where the motto is "shoot first, ask questions later". An extraordinary development.'

'Except when one receives a trigger warning first, I suppose?' I put in.

Holmes chuckled. 'Indeed. A term I had never thought much about before – it has no application to me, after all.'

Now it was my turn to chuckle. 'Oh, but Holmes, surely we all have sensitivities. Do we not?'

A steeliness came into his expression, which I dreaded. 'You are including me in this?'

'No, no . . . perhaps not. Forgive me, Holmes. Talking

of intolerances, I should have remembered how tarragon affects my tummy. Thank god that we are here, back at the cottage . . .'

And hoping that I had successfully avoided a small conflict with my dear friend, I unlocked the door. At the same time thinking, disloyally, that if the famous detective had a trigger, perchance it was receiving criticism . . .

14

After we returned to the cottage I was glad to end the conversation and so failed to ask Holmes to explain his solving of the case. When he was ready it would pour out, and in the meantime I could move my mind to having what I most desired, which was a few days' holiday.

Sat in the choicest armchair, I had begun to plan a few outings and activities, and to consider which of the local restaurants appealed to me most, when a sudden urge to close my eyes for a moment came over me.

The next thing I knew, Holmes was standing there pulling on his coat and calling on me to 'Stop snoring and look lively! We're going out – an evening in Grimpen awaits!'

Flustered, I put on my coat and followed him out of the door. He said there was a local event we must attend. My dear friend had made himself practically a world expert in many fields: paper manufacture (and its geographical origins), perfume ingredients, and he could identify every type of cigarette and cigar tobacco from the ash alone (with the help of his trusty magnifying glass). But he was *not* at the forefront of current technology. Hearing about local happenings on Twitter was certainly not his modus operandi.

'Where are we going, Holmes?'

'A local protest meeting. We are sure to learn much.'

'And how did *you* find out about it?'

'On a little device called the wireless, my friend. You

must try it sometime – marvellously useful contraption.' He was striding down the garden path while I still struggled with my coat.

'I thought you had cracked the case?' I asked, pulling the door to behind me.

'Oh, indeed – but there are many details to clear up. In particular the exact *identity* of the culprit. I have sent a letter to our friend Ms Sholdsmith telling her we will see her in the morning to clear everything up.'

'A letter, Holmes?'

'Indeed.'

Considering the state of heightened distress we had left the young woman in, it did not seem the most caring course of action towards our client to leave her unapprised until the following morning. I fished out my phone, and sent a text to reassure her that a breakthrough had been made.

'Are we not walking?' I asked. The sun was low over the moor, and it was not as warm as earlier, but I could not face another wait for Ted's taxi. A familiar cheery honk, however, informed me that Holmes had thought ahead.

'Booked it forty minutes ago,' he said. 'Didn't see any need to wake you – you looked so peaceful, my dear chap! This rascal's getting slower though, isn't he . . .'

The protest meeting, when we reached it, was considerably larger than I had expected. Perhaps a hundred or a hundred and fifty people were gathered in front of the sandstone council buildings, placards raised, chanting so loudly that we could hardly hear Ted's request for 'five of your English quid, cheers, geez!'

'I'm starting to tire of that man's insulting bonhomie,'

Holmes said – or at least I think he did. It was hard to hear over the hubbub.

'I beg your pardon, Holmes?'

He took me by the arm and we retired to a position where we could watch the crowd, without being mistaken for part of it.

'We demand a right to roam!' a thirty-something woman was yelling through a loudhailer. The crowd loudly agreed with her. 'Hundreds of square miles of Dartmoor National Park are free to roam but blocked off by private land belonging to millionaire hedge-fund managers!' A roar of approval greeted this.

A television camera crew was recording the event. However, after ten minutes the noise died down and from the throng a separate group came forward, with a different spokesperson, this time a neat middle-aged man in glasses. We watched as the camera crew repositioned themselves to shoot from a different angle, and the loudhailer was passed over.

'They're making it look as though the protests happened on different days,' Holmes said into my ear. 'Rather clever, is it not?'

'The cuts this government has imposed on local communities are a disgrace!' the man cried. There was a loud chorus of approval. 'What more can they take away from us? Our libraries have closed, our bus routes been cut off! And the cost of living is going up every day! All we want is basic living standards for ordinary people!'

'Fascinating,' I said. Holmes inclined his head to show that he agreed.

After this, with the TV crew again shooting from a

different angle, another group came forward to take a stern position on a new Amazon warehouse and a bypass which had been approved – to be built through a stretch of ancient woodland, destroying the habitats of hundreds of rare species.

'According to my mobile telecommunicational device, the nearest Amazon pick-up point should be exactly here.'

A robust older fellow with a shaved head began making a speech about large numbers of illegal immigrants being housed in local hotels, which was agreed with by a fervent minority, but by now the crowd had begun to melt away and the TV crew were recording with visible reluctance.

'Clever fellows have got themselves a week's worth of local television reporting right there. Good old organized activism!' said Holmes. 'Now, let's follow this crowd . . . I feel the key to our mystery is shortly to be in our hands . . .'

15

The crowd did not decamp far. Only a few hundred yards down the road there was a little side turning, and we found ourselves crammed into an outdoor area beside a quaint little construction like a disused sweet shop, over whose front door was a hand-painted sign declaring it a 'Micro-Brewery'.

Holmes and I elbowed our way in, past an umbrella stand for discarded placards on which was written 'PLEASE LEAVE POLITICS AT THE DOOR'. (The stand was presumably a permanent fixture, as signs reading 'Countryside Alliance' and 'Just Stop Oil' rubbed shoulders with 'Vote Brexit' and 'No Poll Tax!'). The whole bar consisted of a plank of wood, behind which were four steel barrels on a rack, and a harassed-looking man who I recognized as the leader of the 'Right to Roam' contingent.

Into a space about adequate for six humans, thirty adults had squeezed themselves. Over the tumult of several dozen voices, I caught tantalizing phrases such as 'Baskerville Hall . . . a matter of time', 'bloody greenwashing . . . no smoke without fire, of course', 'lights on the moor . . . last few nights, I saw it too . . .' – but, turn and squirm as I might, I could not locate the speakers to inquire further.

'I say,' said Holmes. The harassed-looking barman didn't hear him. Several more attempts also proved in vain, and so we settled to wait patiently, crammed into the bar's furthest corner.

'Holmes,' I said. 'I feel I've been of little use to you so far in this case, and so I've been doing a little research into the trigger of the gun we saw. I believe it is a historical piece, probably of Damascus steel, possibly pre-1900, and almost certainly a twelve-bore breach-loading gun. My searches indicate either a Henry Atkin model or a James Woodward, both popular . . .'

'Watson, you are correct!' said Holmes. I looked up at him in surprise. 'It *is* a twelve-bore. But in fact it is a Holland & Holland, from 1911.'

'Holmes!' I said. 'How did you . . .'

'While you were giving yourself dyspepsia by devouring a chicken pie with tarragon at the Hound Inn, I was examining the fine firearm above your head. Which, I noticed, was without its trigger.'

I cursed myself for not having noticed this myself. It was always most galling, after so many years by Holmes's side, to fail to follow his most basic instructions of taking in all around you.

'That wasn't the only thing I noticed. The menu, Watson.'

I struggled to recall it.

'It offered "panninnis" with "French freis", and for pudding – which came under a header reading "deserts" – a most extraordinary-sounding dish: "strawberry mouse". Do you fancy tucking into a strawberry mouse, Watson?'

'I am an adventurous eater, as you know, Holmes,' I said. 'But there I think I should have to draw the line.'

'Quite. Then think of the misspelled graffito – "murderes". Was it supposed to say "murderers", or "murderess"? We can find out by asking whoever wrote that menu, I suspect. Not enough to convict in a court of law, but I feel certain the mystery of the trigger and the vandalized sign is solved. The traditional locals fear what Baskerville is becoming; they want a dreary old ruined hall back so they can get tourists in to play on their Hell Hound fruit machines, and get funny tummies from their pies.

'The locals have their doubts about this brand-new eco-friendly character for the place. Their business model is still oriented around the Gothic mansion and the vengeful hound, after all. If this new fashionable Grimpen becomes the centre of a political row, and is humiliated, then no one will come here. It will be scrubbed from the map – "cancelled", as surely as the local bus services from Buckfastleigh and Tavistock have been. Best get the place closed down as soon as possible, destroy that business. Preferably it should lie in ruins. *That* is what they want.'

'But this can't be right . . . !' I protested. 'They are destroying their own livelihood!'

'At first glance, yes – but think about it. There is a demonic intelligence behind the scheme. Why did the hell-hound appear in the first place? *For vengeance!* To protect the virtue of a helpless working-class girl against the rapacity of the privileged lord and his friends, in 1647. And in the public imagination, it was for some supposed similar reason – although you and I know better – when last we visited Baskerville and the Grimpen Mire.

'The hell-hound only appears when terrible injustices need to be redressed. If historical accusations, justified or otherwise, cause the new business at the Hall to fold, and there are sightings of the hound to boot, then in the public consciousness the hound is back and locals have nothing to worry about. If the Hall should fall into ruin again, how much the better!'

'And all these sightings of a giant hound are a fabrication?'

'Of *course* they are! At my most generous, I might concede they could be the result of autosuggestion or wishful thinking . . .'

'Or collective neuroses . . .' I put in.

'At a *push*,' said Holmes. 'You see, the perpetuation of this superstitious myth is their bread and butter – just as the Loch Ness Monster must be essential to any number of lakeside enterprises in its part of Scotland.'

I began to understand what he was driving at – yet so many questions remained.

'The letter, the defacing of the sign – both could be swiftly done,' I said. 'Toppling a statue, though . . .'

'There we come to our *second* culprit, Watson. A much more dangerous and disturbed individual. And someone who – I'm sure you noticed – can spell. He knows the difference between "your" and "you're" when scrawling abusive messages. I refer you to page four of the aforementioned newspaper: the tractor stolen from a farm two weeks ago has been recovered in some woodland.'

The little bar, which had so evidently been someone's front room until very recently, was free of almost any adornment, but along the shelf to our side were piles of leaflets referring to local businesses and attractions. Holmes reached over and plucked up one which showed walking routes across the moor.

'Let us triangulate,' he said, spreading the map out. 'Baskerville Hall is here. The farm from where the tractor was stolen was said to be – let's see – about *here*. And the wood where the thing was discovered was . . . yes! Clearly marked, how helpful. Now . . .'

I watched, dazzled, as he swiftly drew circles on different sections of the map and then held it up for us to look at.

'I don't know about you, Watson, but if I were a criminal hiding out on the moor, who wanted to attack the Hall – here – having stolen a tractor from the farm – *here* – I would dump it as far from my hiding place as I could, so as to prevent prying eyes. My guess is therefore that our mysterious assailant is to be found somewhere within this parameter . . .' And so saying, he drew a swift circle and tapped the middle of it with his pencil.

I gasped. 'Holmes,' I said reverently, 'I think you may be right!'

16

'What's that?' he asked. 'It's a din in here. Speak up, Watson!'

Before I could do so, I felt a pressure on my arm and found myself looking into the anxious face of Madeleine Critchley.

'*Damn* these DFLs!' she said, returning a shove she had just received from some solicitor or account manager. 'It's mostly these leisure-rich dickbags who've got time to go to protests in the first place . . .'

'Ms Critchley!' I said. 'You seem distressed. Can Holmes provide you with a soothing tonic of some sort? He's at the bar now . . .'

'Never mind that,' she said in a rush. 'Dr Watson, I'm so glad to find you – something terrible has happened. Bernie Sholdsmith has gone missing!'

Holmes had been looking decidedly pleased with himself and, turning aside to try to order a drink, had finally managed to get the attention of the activist barman. 'A sherry! Any kind,' he had said, waving a five-pound note, to which the barman had replied that he could offer him beer, beer or beer. And also that he did not accept cash. Holmes's spine stiffened while these effronteries sunk in, before he realized what he had just overheard – and now the great detective turned around as if stung.

'What!' he cried.

'She hasn't returned home this evening. No one has seen her since this morning – her phone has been switched off . . .'

I checked my mobile telephone to see the message I had sent her. Indeed – it had not been delivered, and I had no coverage at all. Holmes looked grey. 'This is all my fault,' he said.

'You up?'

'Yeah mate, so what's your order?'

'I must use your telephone at once!' said Sherlock Holmes.

The barman blinked tiredly. 'I'm sorry, I can't give that out to customers – my whole business is on my phone. I can't just hand it to any Tom, Dick or Harry.'

'But our names are not Thomas, Richard *or* Henry. I tell you, it is a matter of life and death!'

The barman looked between Holmes and me. 'Oh, I get it,' he said. 'You're on one of those themed detective weekends. Solving a mystery, are you – dressed up as Sherlock Holmes and Dr Watson. Well, have fun. I've got customers to serve.' And he vanished along the bar, behind elbows and bobbing heads, to dispense craft ale.

'Imbecile!'

'No one has coverage round here,' Madeleine said. 'The whole of Grimpen is an awful blind spot. It might be better in the middle of the village . . .'

17

We reached it at a run, and found . . . still no coverage. But the post office was open.

'Thank goodness,' said Holmes, leaping for the door. 'Madam! I must send a wire of utmost urgency!'

'A what?' said a kindly-looking bespectacled woman behind the counter.

'A wire – a telegram. It is of crucial importance!'

'We haven't done those since 1982,' she said patiently.

'Foiled again by these petty despots,' said Holmes savagely. 'Make no mistake, I've got my eye on you! Fingers out of the till, you villain!'

'Oh dear, oh dear,' I said, covering my eyes, as Holmes strode outside to a telephone box.

'What's this?' he cried, his frustration nearing a pitch of frenzy. He was clutching the paddles of a defibrillator. The coin-operated telephone once housed in the box was long gone, replaced with life-saving medical equipment.

'My dear Holmes, put those back, and calm down, or we'll be using them on you!'

Swearing vengeance on the privatisation of British Telecom, Holmes strode off down the street. Madeleine Critchley was still with us, and as alarmed as I was at my friend's impetuosity. She assured me she would contact the police from her landline at home, and set off at once.

'I've been guilty of the terrible crime of complacency – I cannot believe I have been so short-sighted, and so stupid,' Holmes grumbled as I struggled to keep up with him.

It was nearly an hour later, and we were marching home through the encroaching dusk. The intervening time had done nothing to improve Holmes's mood. Mere moments after we had set off on foot, a car had swept past us and honked its horn. It was none other than Ted's taxi.

'Hop in, gents?' he'd asked.

When he inquired after our dark despairing attitude, we elucidated the case to him as far as we could.

'Oh yeah?' he said. 'Everyone thinks they're a detective these days, don't they? I've been watching that *Shetland*. Now *that's* a good show . . .'

'We actually *are* detectives,' Holmes said icily.

'Really?' he said, spinning to look at us as the car swerved jauntily from one side of the road to the other. 'I thought you was that couple of artists. You know – Gilbert and George. Tried much detecting before, have you?'

Holmes closed his eyes and ground his teeth.

'Er, yes . . . a good deal in fact . . .' I put in diplomatically.

'Oh well. Can't win 'em all. You'll solve a case one of these days, I bet – keep at it . . .'

'My track record speaks for itself, sir!' said Holmes.

'Oh really? What does it say?'

'It says *I am Sherlock Holmes*, you blithering half-witted oaf!' he exploded.

Which explained why we were now trudging along a darkening path and trying to work out from the memory of our glimpses through the window of Ted's cab whether we were really taking the correct route. The going was muddy, and getting worse.

'I believe we may have taken a wrong turning, Holmes,' I suggested.

'It *is* this way,' he said stubbornly. 'It must be. Why, a glance at the stars alone indicates . . .'

He looked over my shoulder, then turned to stare along the path ahead. I could see a distinct expression of indecision in his mien. But I knew just as surely that he would not own up to it.

'This way,' he said, and returned to his former path. I knew I was no brilliant navigator, but I was increasingly convinced we were on the wrong track. I hesitated.

'Come along, Watson!' he called over his shoulder. I hesitated still.

'Don't dither, man!' he called again, his voice a little fainter.

I felt the cold creeping in through my flimsy waterproof. I was thinking hard about our route, and felt I knew where we had gone wrong – a quarter of a mile back, where we had briefly debated our course. If I hesitated about anything, it was in wondering how exactly to disagree with Sherlock Holmes while he was in such a dudgeon.

I opened my mouth to call to him, and stopped.

For as I went to speak, a howl rang out.

A distinct, keening howl, that of a very large dog. It was loud, piercing and incredibly near.

'Holmes – I see strange lights glimmering in the darkness across the moor. What nefarious activity can this betoken?'
'You're pointing it the wrong way, Watson.
That's the local Wetherspoons.'

18

Sherlock Holmes happened to be turning at this moment, either to cajole or threaten me into following him.

I saw his eyes go wide as saucers. He turned first one way then the other, unsure which direction the sound had come from. I distinctly saw his hands shaking like leaves in a high wind, and his mouth sagging open involuntarily.

Never had I seen my friend express such utter and uncontrollable terror as in that moment. All the horror of our previous excursion upon these moors must have been resting in his subconscious these many decades. At this single sound it came rushing to the surface and overwhelmed him with fright.

Unable to control himself, Holmes ran on shaky legs in the other direction. I saw at once why he had been turning to call to me – he was at the top of a rise, about to jump down. Which he now did – quite out of sight.

The howl came again – closer to Holmes than to myself, it seemed to me, and getting closer by the second. To follow him was to run towards danger.

Thus I turned and made in the opposite direction at the top speed I could muster. I did not think. I scarcely breathed. I only focused on the one goal, that of bodily protection and survival.

When I gathered my wits, I was crouched shivering and breathing hard on the other side of a stile. The howl came again, but it was far behind me. I had no idea what to think – had I done the right thing? Was Holmes safe? Would I ever see my dear friend again, or had I abandoned him to death on the moor?

I entertained all these doubts as I walked. I soon found myself on the right way again, and realized I had been correct all along about the route. And not too long after this, the thatched roof was in front of me – and the front door – and my bed – and oblivion.

19

The following morning I awoke with a start. Shaken by the previous evening's events, I checked Holmes's room – it was empty. My doubts and self-recriminations swarmed in on me again.

But a survey of Holmes's belongings gave me pause, and I went down to breakfast thoughtful. It was clear to me from what was left in his room that Holmes had been wearing several layers of clothing, and had taken his knife with him, not to mention a few choice toiletries.

I was no great detective (as he was all too fond of pointing out), but these preparations on his part made me wonder if he had been secretly planning for some such eventuality. After all, attending a village protest and making a visit to a micro-brewery required no such forethought.

I thought about this as I joylessly consumed the small portion of muesli which had been provided in an individual cardboard packet. It did not satisfy me, but neither did it make me desire a second portion.

I left the house somewhat unsure of my destination and found myself automatically wandering towards the end of the lane, where another small house came into view around the edge of a wall.

I approached up a pretty garden path and knocked politely on the door, receiving no response. On the off chance, I walked to the back garden and peeked my head around.

The sun was bright and the garden was in full splendour, a fountain splashing from the mouth of a stone boar into a miniature fish pond. Beside it was a woman of perhaps seventy-five, with grey curly hair, sitting back in a chair and reading *Five on Brexit Island* with evident pleasure. At my approach she smiled and put the book down.

'I hope you don't mind . . .' I said. 'I'm staying up the road, you know . . .' I explained that I had been asked to investigate some unfortunate events at the Hall. '. . . and I was told that the heir to the Baskerville estate lived here? Might I meet them?'

The woman smiled again. 'She's in there,' she said, nodding towards the patio door. 'Go in, she won't bite.'

I thanked her and entered with a sense of mystery. Inside was a prettily appointed living room decorated to the taste of a retiree, but with no occupant. Then the sound of a television took me to a door and I peered into what seemed to be a games room. A girl of ten or eleven sat on a beanbag, with a video game controller in her hand.

She looked up at me without any curiosity whatever.

'I'm looking for the heir to the Baskerville estate,' I said.

'That's me,' she replied. 'What do you want to know?'

20

I sat on a sofa at the side of the room, unsure where to start. The girl told me her name was Sookie. That she could not attend school at the moment due to suffering from anxiety. That the lady outside was her great-aunt Beatrice.

All the time she played a brightly coloured game, controlling a cutely animated dog which leapt upwards from branch to branch of a seemingly endless tree, collecting coins and diamonds that spun in the air invitingly.

'When did you sell the Hall?' I asked.

'Two years ago,' she said. 'As soon as my uncle was declared dead.'

'I'm sorry about that,' I said.

'I'm not. He sounded horrible. Never met him, anyway.' Her eyes didn't leave the screen.

'Some people seem to have got into their heads,' I said carefully, 'that there is something wrong with the way the family made its money.' I cursed myself as soon as I spoke, for what was an eleven-year-old girl supposed to say to that? It was a perfectly stupid conversational gambit.

'Oh yeah,' she said. 'That was me. I started all that.'

'You didn't!' I said. 'How – why?'

'The concept of a landed gentry is outdated,' she said casually. 'And inherited wealth is disgusting. Money should be shared equally among all sections of society. That's perfectly obvious.'

'I . . . but . . .'

'It doesn't make any difference how any one or other rich family made its money. They are all more or less equally complicit in cycles of oppression and maintenance of an abusive status quo. I don't want my family's money, or to live under the . . .' She paused the game, and looked up at the ceiling, picking the right word. '. . . the *suspicion* of enjoying it, or that I'm virtue-signalling by giving it away. So it's better for me that it appears tainted. Which it is for me already, just by existing.'

'So the family never invested in oil, so far as you know?' I asked, and scarcely believed I asked it.

'Oh sure. Back in the seventies and eighties they did. But so did everyone back then. They were the soundest investments on the planet. Actually the family were pretty ahead of the curve – I know all this because I've had to learn all about their investment history recently. They got out of it in the early nineties as the first news about global warming and its connection to oil sunk in. I bet my uncle hated that. He was as oily as they come. From what everyone says about him.'

She glanced a smile at me and then carried on playing. Her little character continued to leap upwards, never missing a branch. With each coin she collected, there came a pleasant ringing sound, like a tiny bell.

'You don't object to accumulating riches in this game,' I pointed out.

'It gives a sense of achievement,' she said. 'But in this game, you see, I didn't start out with a million coins in the bank. I started out with nothing. That's the fun.'

I nodded, watching her character on the screen jump

and jump and jump. I felt as though my own world view was strangely simplistic, and that I had just been taught something obvious.

'You're not a very ordinary little girl, are you?' I asked.

'In what sense?'

'I mean – how did you educate yourself in this manner? Where have you been schooled?'

'I told you – right here. I get panic attacks in school. I do remote learning. But what I know about politics is mostly from YouTube.'

'YouTube, by Jove!'

'Oh yes. Don't mock. There are lots of very interesting visual essayists with persuasive points of view, once you start looking. I think you would be very surprised.'

'I would indeed,' I said. 'So you are a – a socialist?'

'Yes, I'd say so – although that's rather a loaded and outdated term, I get the feeling. Anyway, inherited wealth disgusts me. So I've turned it down.'

I had hardly dared to think I might get to the heart of the issue of the Baskerville finances while talking to a little girl whose eyes were glued to her Nintendo Switch. Yet now my mind quickened, for we were getting to the heart of it indeed. I mastered my amazement and forced myself to ask in a calm voice: 'How did you do this interesting thing?'

'Took ages. Was really boring,' she admitted. 'I liquidated all the estate's assets – sold the buildings, I mean – then put all the money in a trust and divided it up between carefully chosen progressive green charities. Ones which get a high rating in "Ethical Consumer". We're in the final stages of disbursal at the moment. It's taken years, as I say. Boring old paperwork, and all my decisions have to be ratified by an adult, who luckily enough for me – and the charities – agrees with everything I've done.'

'And you've allowed people to think – wrongly – that the family made all its money from the oil trade?'

'Yes, that suited me. So that my friends – mostly the other home-ed kids who I hang out with remotely – sympathize with me because of the family shame, instead of resenting my privilege.'

'There's no whisper in all you've found out that there's a family connection with . . . slavery?'

'No! Don't be stupid . . .' A frown of irritation creased her face, but vanished in an instant. Suddenly she punched the air, looked at the ceiling and gasped with relief. 'Finally! Oh, I can't believe it. That level's been killing me.'

'Sookie?' came a voice from the living room. 'Are you nearly finished with your maths? It's time for history soon . . .'

She turned off the Switch with her controller. She reached out one foot and flicked open a laptop on the floor in front of her, then pressed the on button with her big toe.

'Party's over, I guess,' she said, smiling at me.

21

I retreated along the lane, pondering this new information, and wishing I could share it with my dear friend, the famous detective. I stood at the turning which led onto the moor and thought for a moment.

Although I was a little reassured that Holmes was a hardy character and would most likely survive on the moor (as he had in former times, and much more difficult circumstances, for many weeks on end), the details of our separation were undoubtedly perturbing.

Reaching in my pocket, I drew out the map which Holmes had scribbled on the previous evening. I stopped and looked at it, then an idea struck me. After consulting a little compass I kept in my top pocket, I set out across the rocky plain, map in hand.

It was early and I was in good physical shape. I felt I had a better-than-decent chance of finding the spot Holmes had marked, which I was also certain he would be making for.

I crested several tors, jumped over many streams, and stopped for a breath and to admire the view. An hour passed, and then two more, until long after lunchtime I paused to check against visible landmarks, sure that (if my reckoning was accurate) I must be getting close.

Both Bernie Sholdsmith and Madeleine Critchley had admitted to being mesmerized by 'something' out there on the moor. Some activity, some presence – and a glowing from this spot had been visible the last two nights, as I had myself observed from my bedroom window.

And as I crested the tor which was within the centre of Holmes's pencilled circle, I saw it.

A collection of tents – perhaps twenty or thirty. Several fires with people sitting round them, many of them playing music. Nearest me was a group sat peacefully weaving baskets, while another group beside them chanted. A drumming circle was visible (and audible) further off, and in a marquee to one side fifty or so people lay in prayer or meditation while they were soothed by the peaceful sounds of wind chimes and hand-made instruments.

I hesitated. Stopped, in fact – and turned back, flustered, trying to stuff the map back in my pocket and make as hasty a retreat as was dignified. I was too hasty – I slipped, twisted my ankle and cried out in agony.

22

'You poor man,' said a woman. 'Is that better?'

'Ah!' I said. 'Please forgive me intruding . . . I feel such a fool . . .'

I looked around the tent into which I had been carried on a stretcher by a group of four women. All were friendly, and frankly amused by my embarrassment.

'What is . . . where am – I mean what are . . .'

'What are we doing here?' asked the woman who was tying a bandage tightly round my ankle. 'It's a women's festival. It's secret – sort of – not much of one, really. We gather away from the world, and from *men* . . .'

'I really am so sorry!' I said.

She burst out laughing. 'We have no permission to be here. That's half the fun! You've got as much right to be here as I have. We don't care. We're here to worship the moon and do what we like and sing and be together.'

'But about one in three of you is, um . . .'

'Yes, there's lots of nudity. That's also part of the fun. If we don't care then neither should you. What were you doing here? There's lots of weirdos out on the moor, you know. You ought to be careful going out on your own . . .'

'Funny you should mention it,' I said. 'I was looking for someone. Who's not a weirdo exactly, but . . .' I wondered how to describe Sherlock Holmes. 'Well, he's not your average sort of fellow either.'

'You've come to the top of the wrong tor, I'm afraid, Mr . . .?'

'Watson. I'm a doctor.'

'Ah – then how do you rate my nursing, may I ask?'

'How did we do? Please rate your experience with us today!'

'Top notch. I am most grateful. Now I must—'

'You're not going anywhere for a few hours. That ankle needs to rest. Here . . . let me find you a stick to lean on . . . and I'll get you a hot drink.'

I was still bright pink with shame and mortification at having walked in on such a gathering, like some prurient prowling criminal. I accepted the paper cup of chai (a drink which brought back memories of my time in the Hindu Kush) and struggled to my feet.

I was determined to inconvenience these kind women for not an instant longer than was necessary. I leant on the stick and put as little weight on my bad ankle as I could. I then turned out of the door to the healing tent without a single glance towards the gathering.

I could smell there were food stalls, dispensing home-made snacks and bowls of chickpeas and lentils. Someone nearby was telling stories to a crowd, with a lot of audience involvement, and there was a group-singing session somewhere else. All over the assembly was a feeling of peacefulness which I envied, as I felt at the same moment (a tad poignantly) it could only exist if I was not a part of it.

'Tell your fortune, dearie?' asked a voice nearby.

Hunched over in a space between tents was a little lady, with a circle of stones around her. 'Step inside the circle, and I shall read your future.' Her head was covered all over with a blanket so that there was only a small gap for her to see out of. She had heard me approaching but did not yet see that I was most decidedly non-female.

I froze in terror, and in that moment the old lady sneezed and, in a gruff male voice, muttered: 'Oh, *drat* this blasted pollen!'

I gasped. I looked again at the stick I was walking on; it had caused me a moment's surprise when first handed to me, and I realized that not only did I recognize it, I knew it thoroughly – for it was I who had bought it for a very dear friend.

I sat down in the stone circle and said as forcefully as I could without being overheard: 'Holmes! What are *you* doing here?'

'Ah,' said my friend's voice from under the blanket. 'Watson. What took you so long, my dear fellow? Thank you.' These last two words were in response to my crossing his palm with a much-needed antihistamine.

'"Fellow" being the *operative word*,' I said through gritted teeth. 'It is utterly disrespectful of you to infiltrate this charming female gathering. When these kind women find out you're here they'll – well, they'll probably tear you limb from limb! And I shall not stop them!'

'Watson!' he said, straightening to his full seated height. He looked perfectly preposterous. 'I've never seen you so spicy! Who's sneezed into *your* sandwich?'

'Well, what do you mean by scaring me half to death, disappearing into the fog chased by a blasted hell-hound?'

'What was I supposed to do about that? It's not as though I was doing it for fun. It's not a fashionable new exercise regimen by that young Mr Wicks, whose "workouts" you keep encouraging me to watch. Although, that said – I *am* feeling rather sprightly after that bit of cardio . . .'

I took out my hankie and dabbed my eyes.

'My goodness, Watson, you're crying,' he said quietly.

'Oh shut up, of course I'm not. It's just been a trying twenty-four hours, constantly running after you and having to apologize for your awful outbursts. And then not knowing if you were alive or dead . . . What *did* happen?'

'My dear Watson, I might qualify for a free bus pass but I assure you I'm still a fine hurdler! Look here . . .' He stuck one of his legs out from under the blanket. 'I've got

'*Someone* has let the dogs out, Watson, and I'm dashed if I'm not going to discover who!'

the calves of a thirty-year-old. Have a feel! Not like you, tumbling over that hummock. So embarrassing . . .'

I sighed. 'Well, I'm glad to see you are in as fine spirits as ever. You certainly didn't look like you were having very much fun when last I saw you.'

'Hmm,' he said, cocking his head – still inside the blanket, and looking more preposterous than ever. 'There was a moment or two of slight discomfort, I am not afraid to admit it. I roamed the moor all night until at last I found my way here and concealed myself. Without a shred of guilt, may I say, seeing as my dashed life was in danger! What have you been up to?'

I told him, as succinctly as possible. 'This is excellent,' he said. 'It fills in the last few details.'

'I'm so pleased,' I said.

'I am *glad* you're pleased, Watson,' said Holmes.

'I was being sarcastic, as a matter of fact.'

'I know you were, but I was rising above it. Perhaps it's my feminine side coming out in this supportive and nurturing environment. You've been doing fine work in my absence, and I commend you. For you see, I've solved the case.'

'Again?' I said.

'Yes! Properly this time.'

'And what are we going to do about it, sitting here like a couple of Charlies on the top of this hill – me with a sprained ankle and you trapped inside an eiderdown?'

'Watson! Trust in providence. And in Sherlock Holmes. It is simple. First, look behind you.'

I did so. And then I let out a yelp of surprise.

'Ms Sholdsmith!' I said. 'You're alive!'

23

She smiled. Then – just as when we'd first met – emotion overcame her, and she leant forward and grabbed me in a big hug. Unlike many of her fellow festival attendees, she was thankfully entirely clothed, in a rustic dress reminiscent of a medieval peasant.

'I *am* alive, Dr Watson,' she said. 'More than I've been for years! Yesterday, after your visit, I'm sorry to say it suddenly got too much for me. I realized that a job is not worth having your life threatened over, whatever job it is. I just dropped everything. It was the best decision I could have made.'

'It was indeed,' said Holmes.

Bernie looked round, first one way then the other, before her eyes settled on the figure of the supposed fortune teller.

'What the fuck?'

'Step forward, my dear,' said the detective, using his fortune teller's voice once more. 'I shall tell you your fortune.'

She came closer, looking bemused. A hand snaked out from under the blanket and made a beckoning gesture with the forefinger.

'What will you tell me about my future?' she asked.

'How we are going to catch the person who has been sending you death threats, my dear,' said the fortune teller.

'Then I really *am* listening, Mr Holmes,' she said, sitting down. 'Or should I say, "She/herlock"? I thought you were supposed to be a master of disguise? This is *not* particularly impressive.'

'I'd like to see you do better in the dark while stranded in an inhospitable wilderness,' Holmes replied with asperity. '*Dearie.*'

'Stop it, you two,' I said. 'Tell me, Holmes. You said you had a plan. What is it?'

'First we've got to get a phone signal. Then you, Ms Sholdsmith, are going to make a public announcement, and you, Watson, are going to phone Ted's Taxis and make a profound apology . . .'

24

'I shall do no such thing!' I protested, shortly before doing just that thing.

Within two hours Holmes and I were back indoors, and after briefly resting and restoring ourselves were hard at work making preparations.

The following morning found Holmes and myself crouched in a ditch across the road from Baskerville Hall.

'Pass me the binoculars, Holmes?'

'Not yet. Stop wriggling, you're making the bushes move and you'll give us away. There's no sign in either direction.'

'I'm most uncomfortable, Holmes. Is it necessary for us to be secreted like this? This ankle is giving me a sore time, you know.'

'Oh, have some self-control. This is a dramatic moment. Keep calm, and pass me a biscuit.'

'There aren't any biscuits left, just crumbs.'

'What!' he said, shifting over to look in the bag of provisions. The past few days had been trying for both of us, and the last two hours spent hunched in a muddy hole had done nothing to improve either of our moods. The bushes shook thoroughly as he investigated the bag and returned empty-handed to his duty as lookout.

'Crumbs indeed,' he said under his breath. 'Here comes someone. This is it! By jingo, those great individuals of the Post Office are right on time! I always said they were a bunch of bally heroes!'

A van approached, and slowed as it turned in at the Hall. A delivery person got out, and went to press the intercom button. All of a sudden, there was action everywhere.

A figure sprang from the trees to one side of the gates and wrestled the box from the delivery person, who was knocked aside but a moment later back on their feet, shouting: 'Police! You are under arrest!'

At once, half a dozen officers appeared from every direction, all shouting the same thing. But their quarry was fast, and already under the cover of the bushes beyond the van. Panic among the pursuers, as they lost sight of the figure.

'Let us give chase, Watson,' cried Holmes, jumping up.

'Please, Holmes!' I protested.

He put out his hand to help me. 'Fear not, we shall be going at walking pace. He won't get far . . .'

He was cut off by the cry of a hound, which rang out clearly across the treetops. I saw Holmes's hand shake, just as it had done before. He steadied it with a determination of nerve, and I took it gratefully.

Then came a man's scream, a bloodcurdling cry of intense pain and misery.

The two of us walked along until we were at the scene, only a few hundred yards away. Sprawled in a clearing was a man, writhing on the ground, dressed in the clothes of one who had been sleeping rough for weeks or even months. His hands were being cuffed behind his back, while paramedics tended to wounds on his leg. He was shouting and protesting, his eyes swivelling, as he wriggled against the restraints. While we watched, a paramedic injected him with a sedative and he went quiet.

A paramedic, dressed somewhat implausibly, assured us that the villain had been sedated.

On the ground beside him was a giant dog, its chest rising and falling steadily, three darts sticking out of its back and neck. A police dog handler was leaning close over it, looking concerned, stroking its flank.

'You were right,' said a voice. Bernie Sholdsmith stood near us on the edge of the clearing, all of us held back by police officers. 'Who is he?' she asked.

'The deceased heir of the Baskerville fortune – alive again.'

'And how did you . . .'

'Ms Sholdsmith, there is nothing I'd like more than to stand here and tell you all about it. But these officers need to do their jobs. And my dear Watson – he needs to sit down. And possibly a splash of brandy. May we repair to your office?'

As he spoke, the officers carried the offender past. He was half-awake and slurring his speech – nothing he said was intelligible. Then he was gone, in the back of an ambulance, and being driven away accompanied fore and aft by police cars with flashing lights.

'How disturbing,' she said. 'I recognize that man!'

25

'You understand now why he had to destroy the statue of his grandfather?' asked Holmes, from his chair in front of Bernie's desk.

She smiled and shook her head.

Holmes nodded up at the portrait. 'That's where you recognize him from.'

I could see at once he was a kind, jovial
fellow without a care in the world.

She and I both gasped. 'Of course!' she said.

'He knew he bore an uncanny resemblance to his grandfather Charles – but he did not know he also looked like his dastardly ancester Hugo! If he was to return with a new identity then all images of that man had to be removed. So when you released a press statement that a replacement bust was being delivered, exactly replacing the head of the statue that was destroyed, and it would go on proud display inside the Hall, he was driven out of hiding. After all, how could he destroy a bust that was *inside* the Hall without being caught on camera and recognized as the bust's double? Then the cat would be out of the bag!'

'And I suppose he never knew that portrait of Hugo existed?' she said. 'We rescued it out of a corner of the attic quite recently, after all.'

'Exactly – he was hardly ever here his whole life. Childhood in boarding schools, holidays abroad, he must have only visited the place sporadically.'

'And what was his plan?' Bernie asked.

'I want to know too, Holmes! What was going on?'

'He was declared legally dead – well, that's that. I did a spot of research last night; it seems he spent several years in an Iraqi prison for trying illegally to acquire oil fields through corruption. At last he escaped and continued his nefarious activities. He wanted to come home – however there were outstanding warrants against his name. He *could* not return as himself.

'What changed in the last fifteen years, in the petroleum industry? The discovery and proliferation of fracking. He saw a study which showed him the grounds of Baskerville could earn him far *more* if the Hall was destroyed and razed to the ground, than if he inherited it by proper means. Ruin the business, and when National Heritage were forced to sell it, scoop it up for next to nothing. Then, once it was established as a failure and an eyesore, the council would be infinitely more likely to approve a fracking operation – albeit on the quiet, I imagine.'

'So he began a campaign against the Hall?'

'Quite so. Easy enough to do – he only had to call on his skills from the army.'

'How did you catch him, Holmes?' I asked.

'I knew he would have to break cover to steal this bust, which Bernie had told the whole world – via those social medium websites you all use – was being delivered to the Hall this very morning. I insisted the package be brought out into the open, where it would be so easy to steal he could not resist.

'I also suspected the hound would attack him as he made his escape; I remembered – as you will, Watson – the boot that was once stolen from Sir Henry Baskerville *because it had his scent on it*, and then used to make a hound chase after him and try to induce a fatal heart attack.'

'Of course!' I said. 'It was stolen from the Northumberland Hotel, just moments before we visited him!'

'Well remembered, dear friend. I think our culprit recalled the exact same thing, and aware that a new large dog was roaming the moor – which must have alarmed him, you would think, seeing as he was living out there as well – he used one of the products freely available these days to attract the hound towards the outer wall of the estate: scent sprays, they are called. Of course the hound's appearance shocked and alarmed so many of your employees, Ms Sholdsmith, that they started to make up excuses to quit . . . even if, somewhat surprisingly, they all failed to record the hound's appearances on their mobile phones – they must be a diligent bunch who don't keep their phones on them during working hours!

'Well, I decided that two can play that game – I liberally sprayed the box with a similar scent, and hey presto! One criminal captured by one highly intelligent hound!'

Sherlock Holmes humbly bowed his head and accepted our applause.

'That poor dog,' said Bernie. 'I hope it's okay . . .'

'Wait a minute, Holmes,' I said. 'Whose hound *is* this? Where did it come from?'

'You've clearly only looked at pages four and seven of that redoubtable organ, the *Devonshire Beaver*, Watson. Did you not also see a reference to the sentencing of an illegal animal breeder, arrested two months ago, on page thirteen? He claimed in court he was breeding emotional support animals for folks who could not afford them – a defence sure to strike at the heart of any animal lover. In truth he was intending to create new, larger breeds for his own financial ends, selling them to people who desire such illegal and dangerous animals.

'His stock was impounded, of course. But I suspect one animal got away, or rather he set it loose. It was what he regarded as his masterpiece: an enormous super-dog he had dubbed the "XXL Bully". Afterwards, this beast was fed and looked after by a good-hearted but wrong-headed neighbour. See the address of this miscreant?'

Bernie looked abashed when she saw it. 'Oh no! Not Madeleine!'

'Indeed. Your dear friend Ms Critchley was his next-door neighbour. I'm afraid she fed and looked after this outsized canine, which she had seen roaming the moor near her beautiful garden. Just another precious rare animal for her collection. The dog handler who inspected the hound told me,' said Holmes thoughtfully, 'that as an animal bred in captivity, life on the moor was traumatic for her. She only appeared "mad" because she had a painful bite – possibly from one of the wild boar recently reintroduced to Dartmoor. He says if a home could be found for her, there's no reason she couldn't live a happy life. And the dog knows the country round here, after all . . .'

A light of pure happiness had come into Bernie's eyes. 'A wonderful idea! What an addition to the Hall! Thank you!' she said, as she took the slip of paper Holmes offered her, with the details of the dog pound.

'Of course the dog's name is your choice,' said Holmes austerely. 'But I am a firm believer in preserving local tradition. And therefore I feel you ought strongly to consider calling her Mrs Snugglewuggle . . .'

26

Ms Sholdsmith rolled her eyes at this absurd suggestion.

'There are a few other little matters,' said Holmes. 'First, I'm truly sorry to have uncovered that some of your neighbours also participated in these attacks. Of course that was *exactly* what the villain intended would happen. Until Watson and I appeared, the whole thing was going exactly as he planned.'

'It is in your power to turn the evidence over to the police . . .' I suggested. 'It's no better than the illiterate pub landlord deserves.'

Bernie shook her head. 'No, this cycle of accusation and acrimony has to end somewhere. I don't think what he did was wise. Or kind. But I just can't stand seeing another person's livelihood threatened because of one stupid mistake.'

'I suspected as much,' said Sherlock Holmes. 'In which case, I think we can send a strong message by returning the envelope to the Hound Inn, marked "not known at this address". Put it in a letterbox and those redoubtable heroes of the Post Office will do the rest.'

Bernie nodded, satisfied. No more vengeance than this was called for.

'Hopefully now your employees will be emboldened to return,' I said. 'And this enterprise of yours, which Holmes and I both think is a terrific one, can get back on track!'

'I'm so grateful,' she said. 'I couldn't believe that you even came here in the first place – but you've dealt with this matter so brilliantly and so fast.'

'One more thing,' said Holmes. 'Please tell Madeleine Critchley that the mystery of her gladioli is a simple one. She should replant them a good distance from the pond, in *dry* soil and facing south. They should thrive. And . . . I hope you will be very happy together.'

Bernie had been looking relaxed and happy, almost glowing. But this last remark caught her unawares. She stiffened, and looked guarded.

'What do you mean?' she said.

'On our visit to Ms Critchley's house,' Holmes said gently, 'Watson and I both spied a handwritten cardboard sign in an upstairs window. "BE NICE", it appeared to say. A wholesome message. But she proceeded to tell us in no uncertain terms that she didn't like the locals, hated the affluent DFLs – the "down from Londons", Watson – and in fact preferred animals to people. When we saw her at the micro-brewery she said you had not come home, but didn't explain how she knew it.

'The sign in her window was therefore not a sign at all, but a removals box. It didn't say "be nice", but "Bernice" – your name, with the "r" obscured by a window strut. It makes sense that if you introduce yourself as Bernie in this rather high-powered job, "Bernice" is a name you would only allow someone to call you if you are on intimate terms with them. Finally, there is the matter that when Ms Critchley served Watson and myself tea, she gave herself a precise serving of one-and-a-quarter teaspoons of sugar, plus a small bit more. Which you also

On discovering the micro-brewery was card-only,
Sherlock Holmes made his feelings known.

requested in your tea – I've never known anyone else to take such a specific amount. I suspect that one of you has taken up the habit in fond imitation of the other. A small detail that speaks volumes . . .'

Holmes had been looking up at the portrait of the rascal Sir Hugo while he explained this. As he finished, he turned to look at Ms Sholdsmith, perhaps expecting applause or congratulations, as he was used to.

Bernie smiled a more abbreviated and reluctant smile than before.

'You are as impressive as ever, Mr Holmes,' she said. 'But you know, you don't have to announce every one of your brilliant deductions to the world. Perhaps sometimes you ought just to enjoy them in your head.' She leant forward and patted him on the wrist. 'Some people might prefer privacy, after all.'

Holmes said – nothing. He merely nodded with the grave seriousness of a judge who had been corrected on a point of law in his own courtroom. It was a sight I had not seen in a long time – Sherlock Holmes, lost for words!

27

'And you are back to London on the next train, Dr Watson tells me?' Bernie said, returning to her former friendliness, perhaps more by effort than instinct.

'Yes. I feel thoroughly invigorated by my time here in Devon, I must thank you,' said Holmes graciously, the awkwardness of the previous moment already forgotten. 'If you want one last piece of unsolicited advice, I'd cheer your office up by getting rid of that picture of the old ruffian and replacing it with something more pleasing to the eye. In fact, I've had the knitting circle at FemFest working on just such a thing . . .'

'I was wondering who this package was from,' she said, tearing the paper off a rectangular parcel. It disclosed a portrait of a certain famous detective, sucking thoughtfully on (but not smoking) his famous meerschaum pipe.

'Hmm,' she said. 'I'm grateful to you, of course, but I don't know if I want you staring down at me all day every day. Possibly you might cover the hole in the stained-glass window that overlooks the café downstairs . . .'

'Perfect!' said Holmes.

'Our taxi awaits,' I said, consulting my phone after it gave a vibrant shudder.

'Then we must be off,' said Holmes. As we descended the staircase to the main hall, he added: 'Tell me, Watson, how did you make it up with our dear friend the taxi driver?'

'I explained to him that you were in a state of deep emotional distress – you had experienced a psychological trigger. He felt very sorry for you. He has theories about how you can achieve balance in your life through mindfulness exercises. I believe he's looking forward to telling you about them now . . .'

He paused on the stair. 'You utter, and complete . . .' he began.

But then paused. And looked at me, and patted me on the shoulder, and carried on walking down towards the front door, waving his stick in the air as though conducting some imaginary orchestra.

Thanks

I really love these short Holmes and Watson books, but they are written to tight deadlines and I rely a lot on friends and loved ones for advice. It would be unspeakably rude for me not to thank those who've helped: Shyam Kumar and Max Edwards first, as editor and agent. Then Steve Savage, who in my mind is uncredited co-author for all his brilliant ideas. Also Evelyn Conn, Lucy Pessell, Hugh Bryant, Kate Hooper, Yvonne Drummond, Vishal Makin. Also Vincents: Catharine, Roger, Juliette, Henry and Benet.

This little book is dedicated with sincere love and gratitude to Steve Savage.